THE ADVENTU

THE TEMPLE OF

OLYMPUS

Written by Ekaterina Botziou

Cover Design by Fiona Dulieu

Inside illustrations by Ekaterina & Christiana Botziou

First published in the UK in 2019

Text and inside illustrations © Ekaterina Botziou 2019
All rights reserved.
www.ekaterinabotziou.com

Cover Design by Fiona Dulieu
Pearl Planet www.fionadulieu.com

ISBN: 9781792844614

25/11/19

To Milia!
Rocco & Cruz,
Hope you enjoy the book!

from Ekaterina Batsiou Pulalis

For my three mythological monsters

Andreas, Dimitrios, Eleni

x x x

CONTENTS

Chapter One

A Gift for Athena p.7

Chapter Two

The Golden Birthday Party p.15

Chapter Three

The High Priestess p.31

Chapter Four

The Giant Thoon p.41

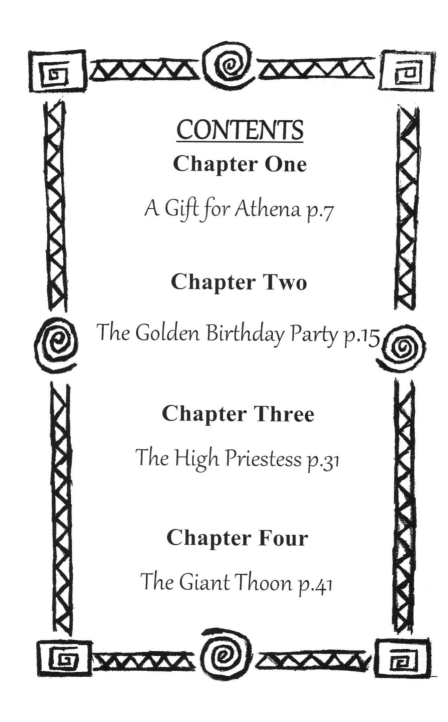

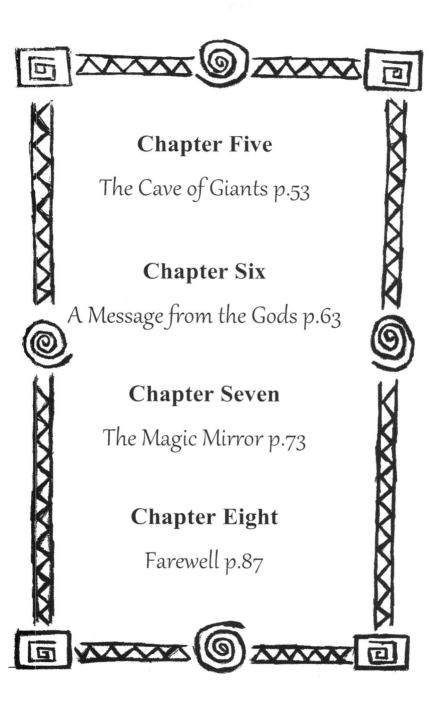

Chapter Five

The Cave of Giants p.53

Chapter Six

A Message from the Gods p.63

Chapter Seven

The Magic Mirror p.73

Chapter Eight

Farewell p.87

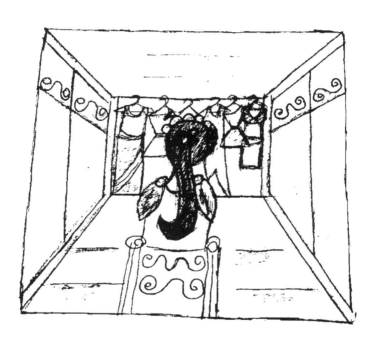

CHAPTER ONE

A Gift for Athena

Athena the Goddess of Wisdom sat sulking. For three days she had sat stubbornly in her room, refusing to join the other gods and goddesses in the golden throne room and only taking food that was left outside her door by her servants.

Tomorrow it was her birthday and still there was no sign of her special present. She flicked a stray cookie crumb off of her pink pillow and stretched herself out flat onto the silk golden bedspread.

"I just don't understand why father won't give me a straight answer," she moaned to her best friend Glaukos the snowy barn owl, who was perched on the end of the bed. "I have been such a good daughter and the perfect Greek Goddess. I'm so much better behaved than Aphrodite and Artemis!"

Glaukos nodded and ruffled her snowy feathers, her talons gripped tightly on the bed railing.

Athena let out a heavy sigh and began twisting a strand of her luscious chocolate brown hair around her fingers. "Father says that I don't need another companion because I have you, but it's only right that you should have a friend too."

Glaukos hooted in agreement and blinked her eyes, then turned her head all the way around and hooted again. "Yes you are completely right Glaukos," Athena smiled. "Of course father won't let me down; he is a man of his word. This and Zeus dismissed him with a wave of his hand.

"Aphrodite will wrap the gift nicely won't you darling," Hera passed the box with the present inside over to Aphrodite who pulled a face. Artemis smirked next to her. Sensing that an argument was brewing, Apollo started to sing loudly at the top of his voice.

"TOMORROW, TOMORROW! Is Athena's birthday! TOMORROW! It's only a day AWAY!"

Aphrodite covered her ears and ran out of the room with the box, whilst Artemis skipped over to the 100 pink doves to check that they were all happy and still pink.

Hera turned to her husband, "Athena will be so pleased with her present, she will think that you are the best father on Mount Olympus!"

Zeus smiled smugly, "Well, I AM the best

father on Mount Olympus! Now back to the checklist. Hermes! Continue!"

CHAPTER TWO

The Golden Birthday Party

The great golden throne room heaved with guests who had come from all over Mount Olympus to wish the goddess Athena a happy birthday. A huge, glittering chandelier hung from the ceiling like a great goblet of shimmering orbs. Sparkly silver and gold balloons floated about in every corner with Athena's face emblazoned all over them.

Against one wall, a long table draped with purple velvet cloth was laden with delicious food. Platters of cherry topped iced buns, shiny red apples dripping with chocolate, ham and cool cucumber sandwiches and a mountain of caramel truffles sat waiting to be devoured. In the middle of the table was a giant birthday cake covered in edible roses and bluebells and adorned with marzipan butterflies.

Water nymphs glided hither and thither offering guests crystal glasses of cloudy pink lemonade.

Apollo and his band '*The Olympians*' crashed about the stage performing one of their latest songs, whilst many of the guests bobbed and jived on the dance floor, swirling and twirling in time to the music.

In the midst of all the celebrating, Athena sat cross legged on the floor in the centre of the throne room, surrounded by her friends and family as they watched her eagerly unwrap her birthday presents. She was wearing a jet black and gold regal robe made especially for her by Queen Hera and her hair was twisted artfully into a Grecian plait.

Uncle Poseidon had given her a beautiful pair of silver dolphin earrings which glinted in the light and she had been presented with a brand new warrior shield made entirely from hydra teeth by her brother Ares. Glaukos the owl was perched proudly on her shoulder.

A huge pile of shiny presents towered beside Athena. Amongst the assortment of jewellery, books and clothes were some more unusual gifts including a very rare golden unicorn named Pegasina. There was also a pair of silver rollerblades with jet boosters and a full length magic mirror which could transport whoever looked into it to wherever they wanted to go.

Lucky Athena had even received a magnificent pair of dragon scale wings from her friend Icarus whose father was a skilled craftsman.

"That's 99 presents and one more to go," Hermes whispered to Zeus, ticking off his checklist. Zeus sat nervously on the edge of his golden throne, watching over the proceedings. Hera sat next to him in a beautiful peacock blue gown, perfectly calm and poised.

Athena carefully began to unwrap her final

present. Aphrodite had done a good job wrapping the mystery package in shimmering gold and purple paper, topped with a triple silver bow. Apollo and his band had stopped singing and now everyone's attention was on the goddess and her special gift.

Throwing the wrapping paper to one side, Athena opened the box and peered inside. A huge smile came over her face as she reached in and lifted out a small mechanical owl no bigger than her hand.

The owl's eyes were made of brilliant amber stone and its feathers were a mixture of bronze and silver metal. Glaukos twit twooed with excitement.

Athena shrieked with delight and jumped up to give her father a hug. "Oh father, he is wonderful! Please please PLEASE give him the gift of life!"

All the guests cheered as Zeus patted his daughter on the head and gently took the owl from her. Pointing his spear towards the owl's head he muttered under his breath, "By the power invested in me as King of the Gods I grant this creature the gift of LIFE!" Out of the end of the spear shot a bolt of lightning and the owl disappeared beneath a cloud of smoke.

Coughing and spluttering, the guests edged closer to see what would happen next.

A strange whirring noise could be heard first. Then as the smoke cleared, two amber eyes shone brightly. The mechanical owl twisted his head all the way around and then blinked three times. "He's ALIVE!" whooped Athena. "Thank you, father!"

Zeus handed his daughter back the owl and watched happily as she danced around the throne room hugging her new friend tightly.

Hera cleared her throat and addressed the crowd of guests, "Thank you all so much for coming to Athena's birthday party and for the gifts you have so kindly bestowed upon her. This special owl is a present from myself and her father. The owl will serve as a friend for

Glaukos and a new companion to Athena. Your Lord Zeus has given him the gift of life. Now I will give him the gift of thought and the power of speech."

The little owl blinked again as Hera bent down and blew into his face. His head whirled once more and he began moving his beak. "He..ll..oo.." he stuttered.

The guests let out a cheer and Athena kissed Hera thank you. Then the other gods and goddesses stepped forward to give the owl more powers.

Aphrodite gave him the ability to love, Apollo bestowed a musical voice, Dionysus gave him merriment, Ares granted strength and magical battle powers and Artemis gave him courage.

Finally, Zeus turned to Athena who stood proudly with Glaukos perched on one shoulder and the mechanical owl on the other. "And what shall you name him my dear?"

Athena thought for a moment, "I shall name him Omicron, which means small." The mechanical owl hooted happily and Glaukos fluttered her feathers.

"Wonderful! Let the celebrations continue!" Zeus signalled to Apollo's band to start up the music but at that moment a piercing scream startled the guests who turned in horror to see a dark menacing figure blocking the entrance to the throne room.

"Have I missed the party?" the figure laughed. "So sorry I couldn't come sooner, my dog Cerberus needed to be taken for a walk." A low growl echoed around the room as the figure stepped forward into the light.

"It's Hades!" the guests gasped.

Hades the God of the Underworld emerged from the shadows, clutching his sceptre. He seemed very tall in his tattered drab black robe and he had a permanent scowl etched on his pale, bearded face. His eyes flashed with anger.

Cerberus, the monstrous three-headed hound who guarded the entrance to the Underworld, snarled and snapped at his master's feet. The beast's three gigantic heads were adorned with a mane of hissing snakes and while his body resembled an enormous black lion, his tale was scaled like a serpent and rattled ominously.

"How nice of you to join us my brother," Zeus feigned delight at Hades' arrival and welcomed him with open arms. "Come and join Athena's birthday celebrations."

Hades smiled to reveal a row of razor-sharp pointy teeth. "No thank you brother, I just thought I'd drop by to give my niece a present but I see she already has far too many."

Athena did not fear her uncle and skipped over to him. "Hello Uncle Hades, have you seen my new friend? Let me introduce to you Omicron the Owl."

Omicron greeted Hades with a whirl of his head but Hades only frowned. "WHAT is that?" he pointed a gnarled finger at the mechanical owl.

Zeus explained, "This is Athena's new companion. Omicron is the latest member of the Olympus family."

Hades grunted and turned to the crowd of guests. "I see you have all become soft up here on your pink clouds," he spat. "Your Lord Zeus knows very well that we cannot let just *anyone* live on Mount Olympus. WE ARE GODS! And ONLY those who are worthy may join us!"

Athena looked worried, "What does he mean

father?"

Hermes butted in, "Well…erm…technically, your little owl wasn't born one of us, he was given powers so he isn't…erm…really part of our clan. The same happened to Hercules. He had to prove his worth before he was allowed to become a god."

"SILENCE FOOL!" roared Hades as Cerberus barked loudly.

Hades snatched Omicron from Athena, "This little owl should NOT be here."

Zeus snatched Omicron back. "As King of the gods, I have the final say not you brother!" he said sternly.

The party guests watched what was happening nervously.

"Erm…but my Lord…Hades is…rrright," Hermes stuttered.

Zeus sighed and looked sadly at his daughter.

"My dear, unfortunately there is some truth in what your uncle has said. I am afraid Omicron will have to go down to the mortal world and prove himself worthy before he is allowed to live with us."

Athena burst into tears and Hera rushed over to comfort her. "Shhh," she soothed, "Omicron is strong and we will watch him from above. He will be set several tasks to complete and when he has completed them he can return to us."

Zeus spoke to Omicron, "Omicron, do you understand that you must prove your worth before joining us?"

Omicron blinked, "Yes Lord Zeus. I will go forth and do whatever it takes to make Athena happy. I am not afraid."

Zeus smiled proudly whilst Hades glared in anger. The guests cheered for the little owl and wished him good luck.

"Then go now Omicron. Your first task is to protect the Temple of Olympus from the giant Thoon. He has been making trouble for the mortals and he needs to be stopped. Go now my friend and may the gods be with you."

Athena kissed the mechanical owl goodbye and Glaukos flapped her wings ardently. Zeus placed Omicron on the ground and pointed his spear at him. The last thing that Omicron saw was a blinding flash of light and Athena's sad face before he felt himself falling down, down, down as the echo of Hades' horrible laugh faded into the distance.

CHAPTER THREE

The High Priestess

Omicron landed with a thump…into a pile of pungent poop. Whirling his head around he caught sight of a grey donkey clip clopping off down the road. The donkey turned and gave Omicron a guilty look.

Flapping his mechanical wings Omicron managed to drag himself out of the dung-heap and looked up towards the powdery blue sky. He had fallen such a long way. But he was sure that he could see Athena waving from that fluffy cloud.

The scorching sun beat down and the air was thick with midday dust. Omicron could feel the dirt starting to cake his metal feathers.

"Where am I?" he wondered aloud. He seemed to be in a busy market place. A row of colourful stalls selling all sorts of food, clothes and jewellery lined the pebbled road and all about him mortals were bustling about. No-one seemed to have time to take any notice of him.

Ruffling his feathers and puffing out his little chest Omicron called out, "Excuse me! I'm looking for the Temple of Olympus!" But nobody even glanced his way.

Omicron flapped his wings and flew from stall to stall. "Erm…excuse me! Could you tell me…? Do you know…?" But the mortals simply ignored him and carried on pushing and shoving and yelling their way about the day.

Exhausted, Omicron set himself down on some cool marble steps, in the shade of a very tall ivory column. He whirled his head around until he grew quite dizzy and shut his eyes tightly to try to help him think what to do.

Just then he heard a gentle voice as soft as silk call out his name. "Welcome Omicron. I have been waiting for you."

Omicron opened his amber stone eyes to see a young girl peering down at him. She was dressed in a flowing white Grecian gown and her chestnut locks were adorned with a wreath of pretty pink flowers.

"My name is Delphina and I am the high priestess of the Temple of Olympus. I am so glad that you are here." The girl smiled warmly.

Omicron bobbed over to the priestess and gave a little bow, "I am at your service oh high priestess. But how did you know that I was coming?"

Delphina giggled. "Oh you are a funny little thing aren't you. The gods tell me things all the time. Your coming was foretold to me."

Omicron blinked. "But where is the Temple of Olympus?" he asked bewildered.

"You are perched right on the steps!" Delphina giggled again.

Omicron turned in awe to find himself sitting right under the entrance to the temple.

The building stood defiantly in the midday sun. It was made up of row upon row of shiny ivory stone columns etched with intricate patterns of the stars.

Delphina led Omicron up the marble stairs and into a large hall that strangely looked very much like the great throne room back on Mount Olympus.

"The temple is modelled on the home of the gods," Delphina explained as she pointed to the large stone statues of Zeus, Hera, Poseidon and all the other Olympians. The statue of Zeus was enormous and was surrounded by weeping candles dribbling with wax. Shrivelled rose petals lay scattered at his feet.

"Do you live here all alone?" Omicron asked, for it seemed like a lonely place to live.

Delphina nodded. "Yes, there is a small room at the very back where I sleep. I spend my days making sure that the statues are protected and sorting out all the offerings that people leave outside the temple. This is only my training though. I am to spend three years here as the high priestess before I can become an Oracle."

"What's an oracle?" Omicron found this all very interesting.

Delphina knelt on the ground next to the statue of Ares and began to polish the marble at the base with a frazzled cloth. "An Oracle can tell the future and predict things that will come to pass. I will have my very own temple so that people can visit me and ask me what the gods have in store for them."

Delphina finished polishing the marble and clambered to her feet. Omicron suddenly noticed a large crack on one of the ivory columns at the front of the temple and another column that had been smashed in half.

"Who did that?" he hooted.

Delphina looked sad. "Those columns were destroyed by the terrible giant Thoon. He is a cousin of the one-eyed giant Cyclops. After the great hero Odysseus killed Cyclops, lots of the giants in Greece have sought revenge. Ever since I came here two years ago, Thoon has made trouble for the people of Athens. Sometimes he just likes to scare everyone and steals food and jewellery. But other times he gets angry and smashes up our homes. The last time he came I refused to come out of the temple, so he hurled rocks at the columns. Lots of people were hurt trying to stop him." A big wet tear rolled slowly down Delphina's cheek.

"So he cannot get inside the temple?" Omicron was appalled at the giant's lack of respect for the gods.

Delphina shook her head, "The temple is

protected but that doesn't stop Thoon from trying to break in."

Omicron thought for a moment. This is what he had been sent here for. This is how he could prove himself worthy of re-joining the gods on Mount Olympus. He must find a way to stop the terrible giant and teach him a lesson.

Without warning, a loud clattering crash broke the silence. The ground began to tremble and the whole temple shook as screams and cries for help rose from the market place.

Frightened, Delphina grabbed Omicron and sprinted to the back of the temple behind the statue of Zeus. She swept aside a thick red velvet curtain to reveal a small wooden door. Reaching into her pocket, she drew out a rusty key and hurriedly poked it into the lock.

"Quick, get inside Omicron! We must hide! It's THOON!" And with that Delphina shoved the mechanical owl into the room and slammed the door shut behind them.

CHAPTER FOUR

The Giant Thoon

The market place was a mess. Stalls had been knocked upside down, carts of food had been abandoned, squashed fruit and vegetables littered the road and everywhere torn clothes and broken bits of ceramic pots were strewn about. The townspeople had fled in terror.

In the midst of the chaos stood the giant Thoon, stuffing three pieces of pita bread into his mouth. "I WANT MORE FOOD!!" he thundered, smacking his lips and licking his fingers.

Thoon was the oldest, ugliest giant in all of Greece and by far the shortest. He had several teeth missing and those that remained were jagged and yellow.

His stringy grey hair was scraped back into a ponytail and his eyes were milky with frost. He wore a dirty sackcloth tunic which fell just above his knobbly knees and he walked with a slight limp. Despite his odd appearance, Thoon was a very dangerous giant and the mortals had tried and failed to stop him destroying their town.

"WHY 'AS EVERYONE RUN AWAY?! ARE YOU ALL SUCH COWARDS?!" Thoon's booming voice echoed through the temple.

Behind the secret door Omicron and Delphina listened.

"We must go out and face him," Omicron said, flapping his wings impatiently.

"We can't!" Delphina cried. "He will crush you and make me his slave!"

Omicron perched himself on Delphina's

shoulder and hooted softly to her. "Thoon is a bully and bullies should not get away with being mean to people. We must teach him a lesson."

"But how?" Delphina looked nervous.

Omicron thought. "Well first we have to confront him."

Slowly, Delphina opened the door just a crack and peered out. They could hear Thoon still crashing about in the market place.

"Right, the coast is clear," she whispered. Omicron fluttered out the door and up to the rafters to get a better view of the giant, whilst Delphina tiptoed behind Hera's statue.

"Can you see him Omicron?"

Omicron flew closer to the entrance of the temple and hid behind one of the smashed columns. The giant was nowhere in sight.

"Be careful!" Delphina warned as Omicron flew out from behind the column and landed on the temple steps.

Suddenly a giant hand closed around him! "GOT YOU!" Thoon dangled poor Omicron upside down and held him up high in front of his face. Thoon's breath smelled like rotting brussel sprouts with a dash of mouldy cheese and Omicron wrinkled his beak in disgust.

Delphina rushed out of the temple, "Leave him ALONE!" she yelled.

But Thoon just laughed.

"AH DERE YOU ARE LITTLE PRIESTESS! NOT SO 'IGH AND MIGHTY NOW ARE YOU? AND IS DIS YOUR TINY FRIEND?"

Thoon flipped Omicron upright and held him tightly. "Unhand me Thoon or you'll be sorry!" Omicron hooted calmly.

Thoon laughed harder than ever. So hard that he started to cough. "UN'AND YOU?" he spluttered. "WHEREVER DID YOU LEARN SUCH POSH LANGUAGE? DID DE GODS TEACH YOU?"

"Yes they did!" shrieked Delphina running forward and kicking Thoon's fat hairy leg. "Omicron was made by the gods to defeat you! Now put him down!"

"OUCH!" Thoon reached out and flicked Delphina with his finger so that she rolled backwards and landed in a dusty heap at the foot of the temple.

A few of the townspeople who had earlier run away peeped out of their hiding places to see who dared try to fight the terrible giant.

"LISTEN WELL PEOPLE OF AFENS!" Thoon spat, growing angrier by the second, his yellow eyes flashing. "YOUR 'IGH PRIESTESS 'AS GOT TOO BIG FOR 'ER SANDALS AND FINKS DAT SHE CAN

DEFEAT ME. BUT SHE IS WRONG! NONE OF YOU CAN STOP ME! AND NOW I WILL EAT 'ER PAFETIC LITTLE OWL IN ONE MOUFFUL!"

"Noooooo!" Delphina screamed.

Omicron thought quickly. Ares had given him magical battle powers but he wasn't quite sure what they were.

A blurred vision suddenly popped into Omicron's mind. It was Zeus! "*Use your powers Omicron. Calm your senses and the magic will come to you.*"

Omicron's head whirled around as the vision disappeared and his body started to tingle. He imagined himself as a ball of flames, like a firework spiralling up into the night sky. His bronze and silver feathers began to glow, softly at first, then brighter and brighter.

Thoon looked confused as he held Omicron in his hand. "WHAT ARE YOU DOING? STOP SPINNING YOUR 'EAD!"

But Omicron did not stop. He twirled his head faster and faster like a dizzy spinning top as his feathers glowed brighter and hotter.

On the ground, the townspeople were now huddled together with Delphina, looking up at the giant and the little owl in astonishment.

"OUCH! STOP BURNING ME!" Thoon screeched. He tried to unclench his hand but Omicron held on, spinning and twirling and glowing redder and redder.

"Dooo yooouuu surrenderrr?" Omicron called out, his voice sailing up and down like the rolling waves.

"NEVER!" Thoon squawked.

With a yelp the giant freed his hand as Omicron slipped out of his grip and fluttered to

Delphina's side. Thoon clutched his smoking fingers and roared in pain.

"LOOK WHAT YOU'VE DONE!" he whimpered, shaking his fists. "YOU WILL PAY FOR DIS!"

He lurched forward but his hand hurt so much that he couldn't keep his balance and tripped over a broken pot.

"AARRRGGGHH!"

"Quickly, get inside!" Omicron circled above as Delphina led the townspeople into the safety of the temple.

Thoon dragged himself to his feet. For one terrible moment, it looked like he was about to charge into the temple columns, but the old giant was clearly tired and thought better of it.

"DON'T FINK DIS IS DE END!" he threatened over his shoulder as he limped away. "I'LL BE BACK WIV MY BROVERS. YOU

WILL BE SORRY!"

Inside the temple, everyone was so relieved that they didn't even bother to cheer. Delphina hugged Omicron tightly and thanked him for saving her.

"The battle has been won but the war is not over yet," Omicron said wisely.

One of the townspeople spoke up. "We thank you little owl. My name is Perimos. I am the mayor of this part of Athens."

Perimos hobbled over to Omicron and patted him on the head. He was old and shrivelled and his wispy silvery beard swept the floor like a broom, but his periwinkle blue eyes twinkled with mischief and mayhem. "I can see that you have been sent by the gods."

Delphina interrupted, "We don't have time to chatter. Thoon will be back soon with his brothers and what we will do then?" She turned to the mayor angrily. "I have asked for your help before but you have just run away."

The mayor looked sheepishly at the floor. "I have tried many times to rally the Athenian guards but King Aegeus needs them to deal with the Minotaur. These past two years I have been powerless."

The rest of the group nodded in agreement and Delphina sighed. "Well now the gods are on our side. Omicron, what should we do?"

Omicron flew up to the statue of Athena and perched on her stone shoulder. He could feel his magical powers growing stronger and knew that Athena and Zeus were watching over him.

"I have a plan."

CHAPTER FIVE

The Cave of Giants

Deep inside a dank, dark cave, Thoon sat sucking his burnt fingers. A small fire sizzled and snapped at his feet, toasting his hairy toes.

"STOP YOUR SNIVELLING!" Thoon's brother Mimas snarled.

"YER, STOP YOUR SNIVELLING!" Thoon's other brother Agrius echoed. He dodged quickly as Mimas angrily took a swipe at him. "STOP COPYING ME YOU FUNGUS FOOTED BUFFOON!" Mimas barked.

All three giants sat huddled around the

glowing fire, bickering about how to defeat their new enemy Omicron the owl.

After fleeing the market place, Thoon had retreated to the cave where his brothers found him muttering to himself and cursing the gods. He told them all about the owl's magical powers and how Omicron had defeated him. The giants swore vengeance.

"SO 'OW EXACTLY ARE WE GONNA SORT 'IM OUT?" Agrius drooled.

Slightly younger than Thoon, Agrius was only a bit taller his brother, with dirty blonde hair plaited down his back. When he was at giant school, he used to play tricks on the other giant children and had spent years frightening them by pretending to roll his eyes back into his head. His mother had told him to stop but he hadn't listened and one day the wind changed and left him permanently cross-eyed. He was also colour blind and wore a pink flamingo-hued tunic slung over one shoulder. He thought it was blue.

"QUIET!" growled Mimas. "I'M FINKING."

Mimas was the youngest of the brothers and by far the most dangerous. He was much stronger than Thoon and Agrius and highly skilled on the battlefield. He had once been in a fight with the demi-god Hercules and would have won had it not been for Ares the God of War interfering.

Mimas ran his hand through his oily black hair which glittered with rattling beads. His skin was thick and scaly and he was clad in iron armour as hard as boiled sweets which he never removed, even when he was asleep.

"YOU SAY WE CANNOT ENTER DE TEMPLE?" he demanded to know.

Thoon nodded. "IT'S PROTECTED BY DEM GODS. I 'AVE TRIED TO KNOCK IT DOWN FROM DE OUTSIDE BUT DOSE

COLUMNS ARE TOO STRONG INNIT."

"SO 'OW WE SUPPOSED TO GET IN DEN?" Agrius scratched his head.

Mimas grunted with annoyance. Pointing his finger at the ground he started to draw some shapes into the dust with his long, rusty fingernail.

"OOO OOO I LOVE DIS GAME!" Agrius sniggled (a snort and a giggle at the same time). "LET ME GUESS WHAT IT IS! IT'S A CIRCLE...NOPE, A SQUARE! OH WAIT DON'T TELL ME!" Agrius clapped his hairy hands together with glee until Mimas thwacked him on the head.

" 'EE'S DRAWING A PLAN YOU NIT WIT!" Thoon scoffed, gazing at the swirl of lines and loops in the dust. "SEE, DERE'S DE MARKET SQUARE AND DAT'S DE TEMPLE. 'AINT DAT RIGHT BROVER?"

Mimas sneered. " 'OW DID I END UP WIV YOUS TWOS AS BROVERS? ONE WIV NO BRAINS AND DE OVER WIV NO BRAWN."

Thoon gritted his crooked teeth in anger and
Agrius looked confused. Mimas sighed and spat
into the fire. The flames shook with excitement
and leapt into the air, casting ugly shadows on
the cave wall.

"WE WILL DRAW DEM OUT FROM DE TEMPLE, INTO DE MARKET SQUARE LIKE BEFORE," Mimas spoke slowly and sounded every syllable so that Agrius could understand.

"IT WON'T BE AS EASY AS DAT BROVER," Thoon snorted. "DAT OWL 'AINT STUPID."

Mimas glared at him. " 'OW DARE YOU QUESTION ME!" he roared.

Thoon bottom-shuffled away from his raging brother and Agrius scuttled to the corner in fear. Mimas snorted and turned back to his drawings.

"AS I WAS SAYING," he went on, "AS SOON AS DE SUN SETS WE WILL MAKE OUR WAY TO DE TEMPLE AND WAIT OUTSIDE. WE WILL PRETEND DAT WE WANNA MAKE PEACE BY MAKING AN OFFERING TO DEM GODS. DE PRIESTESS

BRAT WILL 'AVE TO COME OUT TO
ACCEPT DE OFFERING AND AS SOON AS
SHE DOES…BANG! WE TAKE 'ER
'OSTAGE!"

Agrius slithered back to the fire, a huge grin
on his face. "I LIKE DIS IDEA. CAN I
COME?"

Mimas sighed. "OF COURSE YOU ARE
COMING YOU DOPEY MUPPET. WE ARE
ALL GOING TOGEVER!"

Thoon sidled up to Mimas, licking his lips
with excitement. "AFTER WE TAKE 'ER
'OSTAGE, DEN WHAT?"

Mimas smirked and an evil smile crawled
across his hardened face. "DEN WE DEAL
WIV DE OWL."

The giants whooped and jeered, sure that their
wretched plan would work. They were so
engrossed in their twisted pit of plotting that

they didn't even notice the small ball of sparkling light hovering by, listening intently to every word. Nor did they see it float off out of the cave and flutter towards the direction of the town.

In their arrogance, the giants had forgotten one very important thing: the gods are ALWAYS watching.

CHAPTER SIX

A Message from the Gods

Perimos sprinkled the last few droplets of slippery oil onto the temple stairs and stood back to admire his handiwork. Omicron's plan to booby-trap the entire place was going well.

The special stone polish Delphina used to scrub the statues had been sloshed all over the marble entrance and Perimos had to be careful that he didn't slip over himself.

Some of the townspeople were inside frantically hammering and sawing one of the broken market stalls into a catapult. Others were dashing about the market square, picking their way through pulverized fruits and tangled tunics, trying to find anything that could be of use against the giants.

Delphina and Omicron were speaking to the goddess Athena. Well her statute that is. And she didn't appear to be listening.

"Oh great goddess!" Delphina waved a few more rose petals into the air and threw herself into a sweeping bow. "We beseech you! Your faithful owl Omicron has defeated the giant Thoon but his giant brothers will now come to seek vengeance. How can we stop them?"

The statue remained silent. "Perhaps she does not want to help us," Delphina sighed sadly, a tiny tear threatening to spill from her eye.

Omicron whirred his head from side to side. "I know my goddess. She will help us," he said firmly.

Perimos suddenly staggered into the temple, barely able to contain his excitement. "High Priestess! Omicron! Come quickly!" he panted. "A sign from the gods!"

Everyone scrambled out to the marble steps to see what all the fuss was about. The sun was dipping lower and lower in the sky sending out streaks of crimson red and burnt orange.

Delphina lifted her hand to shield her eyes but lowered it abruptly when she saw a ball of shining light sailing towards them.

"Look there!" Perimos gestured. "The shimmering light is getting brighter."

The ball floated closer and landed softly on the steps in front of them. The townspeople edged forward but were immediately flung back by a cascade of light that burst into flames.

Delphina gasped in awe and Omicron hooted in surprise as the flames died down to reveal a very grumpy looking snowy barn owl dusting the ash from her feathers.

"Glaukos!" Omicron fluttered over to greet his friend. "What are you doing down here?"

Glaukos hooted and fluttered up and down as Omicron nodded and whirred. The two owls looked quite funny jabbering on at each other.

"Who is that?" the townspeople whispered to

each other.

"That's Athena's other owl! The goddess must have sent her with a message!" Perimos whispered back.

Omicron turned to Delphina. "Glaukos has brought a message from the gods! We must act quickly!"

Delphina knelt down by the two little owls. "What must we do?"

Glaukos jibbered and jabbered some more as Omicron translated to his friends.

"The giants will be here by sunset. They plan to trick us and take you hostage."

Delphina gasped in horror. Perimos hobbled forward. "We have set traps outside the temple, they will not be able to get in," he spoke bravely.

Glaukos whirred her head from side to side.

"That won't be enough," Omicron's amber stone eyes grew wide. "If we are to defeat our enemies we must be cunning and use all our powers."

"But what more can we do?" Delphina grew frantic and the townspeople looked very worried. "We have done everything we can. Oh how on earth will we beat them?"

Glaukos fluttered into the temple and perched herself on the statue of Athena. She hooted once more then BANG, the snowy owl dissolved into a ball of light and disappeared into the air.

"Don't go!" Delphina wailed as the townspeople shuffled back into the temple and hung their heads in disappointment.

Suddenly the high priestess noticed something glinting in the setting sunlight and let out a shriek of surprise. "What's that?!" she cried, pointing to a long glass oval shape leaning against Athena's stone legs.

Everyone crowded round to see.

"Blessed be the gods!" Perimos fell to his knees.

Omicron flapped his mechanical wings with excitement. "Athena's magic mirror!"

***

Perimos examined the mirror closely. It had taken four of the townspeople to carry it out to the front of the temple and hide it just next to one of the columns so that they could see it properly in the fading daylight.

A rim of twirled gold encircled the oval shape and two ivory clawed feet stuck out at the bottom. The glass itself was not reflective. It was like looking into a gaping black hole, a limpid pool of never-ending darkness ready to swallow you whole.

Omicron explained that the mirror could

transport whoever looked into it to wherever they wanted to go. But Glaukos had told him that it only worked on Mount Olympus unless someone who had been touched by the gods willed it to come alive.

"But none of us have been touched by the gods," the townspeople muttered to each other.

"Omicron has!" Delphina held Omicron in her arms as everyone turned to look at the little owl.

"The fate of our town lies with you Omicron," Perimos said softly. "We will do all we can to help you but the magic of the gods must come from within."

As he spoke the sun melted into the ground and a velvet blanket of midnight blue draped across the sky.

Without warning, the ground began to tremble and three giant shadows slithered out of the darkness and into the market square. The terrible figures of Thoon, Agrius and Mimas emerged into the dappled moonlight, snarling and spitting like a pack of hungry wolves.

"Quickly! Get inside!" Perimos ordered everyone into the temple as the giants approached.

Thoon's booming voice followed them like a swarm of angry bees. "YOU CAN RUN BUT YOU CAN'T 'IDE!" he bellowed. "WE WILL GRIND YOUR BONES TO MAKE OUR BREAD AND SMASH DE METAL OWL'S LITTLE 'EAD!"

Mimas and Agrius roared with laughter.

Inside the temple Omicron fluttered up to the statue of Athena. He could hear her silky voice whispering in his ear. *"The time is now my little friend. Prove your worth. You can do it!"*

Puffing out his chest Omicron swooped down

to the temple entrance and perched on Delphina's shoulder. "Don't be afraid," he hooted in her ear.

"I am not," Delphina threw her shoulders back and held her head up high. "The gods are on our side."

Beside them stood the mirror, its clawed feet rooted to the spot, silently watching the giants stomping closer. Delphina wasn't sure, but she thought she could hear a faint giggle rise up from the oval darkness. Shaking her head, the priestess narrowed her eyes. This was her temple and no-one, not even a giant, was going to destroy it.

CHAPTER SEVEN

The Magic Mirror

The makeshift catapult was rolled into place in between two columns at the entrance to the temple. It was hidden just enough so that the giants couldn't see it. The townspeople had done a good job constructing it from pieces of broken wooden stalls tied together with an assortment of colourful tunics and sandal straps.

"Load her up!" Perimos instructed. Everyone heaved and ho-d as they piled mushy fruit and squashed vegetables into the bucket. Then they dragged the wooden arm down and secured the bucket.

Omicron and Delphina stood defiantly on the stone steps as the giants leered and jeered at them a few feet away.

"WHY DON'T YOU COME DOWN 'ERE AND WE CAN MAKE PEACE," Thoon drawled, feigning an apology.

"YER." Agrius joined in, wiping his drippy nose on the back of his hand. "WE DON'T WANT NO MORE FIGHTING. WE WOZ ONLY JOKING 'BOUT GRINDING YOUR BONES!"

Mimas said nothing. He eyed the priestess and the mechanical owl suspiciously and tightened his grip on the nasty looking mace he was holding.

"The gods do not make peace with such vile creatures as you!" Delphina's voice quivered with nerves but her gaze was steady. Omicron hooted in agreement.

Mimas growled and dangled a grubby linen pouch which clinked as he swayed it from side to side. "AN OFFERING FOR YOUR GODS," he sneered. "ONE GOLD NUGGET, TWO CRYSTALS AND FREE RUBIES."

"ALL STOLEN OF COURSE," Agrius scoffed. Thoon smacked him round the head.

"OUCH!" Agrius wailed.

"QUIET!" Mimas spat. "SO WHAT IS YOUR ANSWER PRIESTESS? DO YOU ACCEPT OUR OFFERING?" The giants edged closer to the foot of the temple stairs.

Omicron whispered to Perimos who was

hiding behind one of the smashed ivory columns, "Get ready!"

Delphina slowly descended the first marble step with Omicron still perched on her shoulder.

"DAT'S RIGHT," Mimas licked his lips, "JUST A BIT CLOSER AND DE OFFERING IS YOURS…"

Delphina was only on the second step but the giants were already at the same height as her. They could almost reach out and grab her. One more step and she'd be in real danger.

Mimas held out the pouch. Out of the corner of her eye Delphina saw Thoon quickly pass Agrius a long rope, ready to tie up the priestess and hold her hostage. But not today.

Just as Delphina pretended to lean forward to take the pouch, Omicron swooped down and plucked the offering from Mimas' grubby fingers. Taken by surprise, the giants tried to jump up and seize the owl but Omicron was too quick and soared high up into the sky.

"GET 'IM!" Mimas squawked. "AND GET DE GIRL!"

Quick as a flash Delphina turned on her heel and dashed back into the temple. "Now!" she shouted.

Perimos gave the signal and the townspeople launched the first bucket on the catapult. A loud SPLAT sounded as a sloshy mix of rotten tomatoes, purple plums and pimply peaches hit

Agrius right SMACK in the eye as he clambered up the temple steps.

"Bullseye!" Perimos punched his fist in the air.

Momentarily blinded, Agrius squealed in pain and toppled back onto Thoon, who toppled back onto Mimas. The three of them fell to the ground like a line of dominos.

"GER OFF ME!" Mimas bellowed. Shoving his brothers off his back he wielded his mace and thundered up the stairs.

The whole temple shook so much that Delphina was worried the shattered columns might finally give way. But they stood firm.

"Reload!" Perimos yelled to the townspeople who hurried to re-fill the catapult.

Mimas was on the final step to the temple entrance. One more leap and he would be upon them.

WHOOSH! The second round of mashed up fruit flew into the air but Mimas was ready and ducked just in time. SPLAT! Agrius didn't duck and was hit right in the other eye.

"NOW YOU PAY!" Mimas lunged towards Omicron who was hovering just above a big wet puddle of stone polish.

Raising his mace, Mimas took a swipe at the owl but lost his balance as his hairy feet skidded on the oily floor. Bounding up behind him, Thoon and Agrius did not see their brother slip until it was too late.

"AARRGGHH!" Mimas staggered backwards, flapping his arms around wildly. Thoon tried to hold him up, but he tripped over a squashed potato and crashed into Agrius who then slipped on a banana peel.

The three of them skirted and skated on the slippery marble, howling at the top of their lungs until they landed in a heap of bruised limbs and grazed knees.

"BLAST IT!" Mimas bellowed. Untangling himself, he looked up to see a dark oval shape peeping out at them. Scrambling to their feet, the giants peered into the mirror's nothingness.

"WHAT SORTA TRICKERY IS DIS?" Thoon sniffed.

"SHUT YER MOUTH!" Mimas warned. "IT MIGHT BE FROM DE GODS." Mimas wasn't afraid of many things. But if truth be told, he was afraid of the gods.

The mirror was smaller than the giants, but they seemed to shrivel in size before it as the dark gaping hole where a reflection should be stared back at them.

"Use your powers Omicron!" urged Delphina. "Make the mirror come alive! Only you have been touched by the gods!"

Perimos and the townspeople waited with bated breath as Omicron closed his eyes and whirled his head around and around.

"Use the gifts from the gods my little owl…" Athena's gentle voice soothed Omicron's thoughts as he concentrated with all his might on making the mirror come alive.

Suddenly a cascade of bright rainbow colours burst forth from the mirror, flooding the temple steps with a prism of light.

The giants stumbled backwards, dazed and confused.

A deep rumbling noise rose up from inside the mirror, growing louder and louder as it trembled into life. A sliver of silver cracked through the gaping black hole and a pale thin hand reached out. The hand tore the black hole away and crumpled it up into a ball like some discarded wrapping paper.

A swirl of colours shimmered like a kaleidoscope where the black hole had been and a blue-skinned face with hollow eyes and a gaping mouth peered out.

The face yawned. "Whoooo has woken me from my slumber?"

The giants shrieked in fear!

"WHAT IN DE NAME OF TARTARUS IS DAT?" Agrius screeched.

"I am the Mirror of Olympus," the blue face spoke with a voice as rich and smooth as a cream-covered fruit cake laced with chocolate fudge and topped with a shiny cherry. "I transport whomsoever looks upon me to wherever they want to go. Tartarus you say. Are you sure?"

Tartarus was a terrible place where the wicked and the unjust were sent to be punished for their crimes. Many of the enemies of the gods dwelt there in a deep abyss of torment and darkness.

Omicron, Perimos, Delphina and the townspeople watched in awe from behind the ivory columns.

Mimas snarled at the mirror. "DIS IS DE OWL'S DOING! DON'T LOOK AT IT BROVERS! ARE YOU LISTENING?"

But Thoon and Agrius were mesmerised by the swirling colours of the mirror.

"TART…AR..US…" Agrius drooled, hypnotised by the churning shades of blues, greens, pinks and purples.

"Splendid!" the face in the mirror nodded. "And will that be return or one way?"

Before Mimas had time to stop him, Thoon opened his mouth, "WHICH…WAY…?"

"I'll take that as one way then!" the mirror started to shake.

Mimas slapped his brothers hard. "WAKE UP!" he ordered. Thoon and Agrius snapped back to reality but before they could scramble to their feet, a WHOOSHING sound whistled through the air.

A gust of wind spun forth from the mirror, gathering speed as it twisted and twirled, circling the giants so that they could not escape.

Delphina clutched Omicron tightly and the townspeople clung to one another, fearing that they too would be dragged into the whirlwind.

"NOOOOOOO!!" the cries of the giants could barely be heard above the whooshing and shooshing of the gusty spinning top. Faster and faster it span as the giants desperately clung to the edge of the temple steps, their feet flailing in the air.

"Please do not delay," the blue face quipped. In one final flurry Mimas, Agrius and Thoon were sucked into the raging vortex and disappeared into the mirror. The face belched loudly. Then all was quiet.

CHAPTER EIGHT

Farewell

The cheers and whoops of joy were deafening. The previously deserted market square was now filled with people dancing and singing. Chants of "OMICRON! OMICRON!" echoed through the town as word spread of how the owl and his friends had defeated the tiresome Thoon and his brothers.

Omicron and Perimos were helping Delphina to sweep the temple. They may have won the battle with the giants but the place was now a mess and certainly not fit for the gods.

"What was in the pouch Omicron?" Perimos asked as he mopped up the last puddle of slippery stone polish.

In all the chaos, Omicron had dropped the linen pouch the giants had said was filled with jewels. Delphina picked it up and emptied the contents into her hand. A few dirty pebbles fell out.

"So they planned to trick us all along," Omicron hooted. Delphina shrugged. "Never trust a giant," she laughed.

"You have become wise high priestess," Perimos observed with a smile. "You have been very brave and the gods will see that. As for you Omicron, surely you have now proven your worth."

Omicron's wide amber eyes looked sad. "I am not sure," he said in a sombre tone. "I thought that I had done enough to protect the temple. But the gods have remained silent, so now I do not know what else I must do."

"Do not worry my friend," Perimos said kindly. "The gods work in mysterious ways." He shuffled out to edge of the temple steps and gazed up at the stars. At that moment a bolt of lightning streaked across the sky and struck one of the temple columns.

"Delphina! Omicron! Come quickly!" he called.

Delphina rushed out with Omicron fluttering by her side.

"The mirror!" Perimos gasped. "It's gone!"

A loud booming voice from within the temple startled them. "THE MIRROR HAS BEEN RETURNED TO ATHENA. YOU WILL HAVE NO FURTHER NEED FOR IT."

Omicron flapped his wings, "It's Zeus!" he cried excitedly, zooming back into the temple.

Sure enough, the statue of Zeus was radiating a godly glow but his lips did not move as he spoke.

"YOU HAVE DONE WELL MY LITTLE FRIEND."

Delphina and Perimos bowed down at the statue's feet.

"HIGH PRIESTESS, YOU HAVE DONE WELL TOO. COMPLETE YOUR TRAINING AND YOU WILL BECOME AN ORACLE IN NO TIME," Zeus continued. "AND MAYOR PERIMOS, YOU ARE ALSO TO BE CONGRATULATED. LOOK AFTER THIS TOWN AND YOU WILL FOREVER BE REMEMBERED AS A GREAT MAN."

Delphina and Perimos smiled proudly. Perimos cleared his throat, "Oh great Zeus," he spoke politely. "We merely did as Omicron instructed us. He has been a very brave owl."

Omicron looked bashful but hooted gratefully.

Zeus glowed even brighter. "OMICRON

HAS COMPLETED THE FIRST TASK I SET HIM AND ATHENA IS VERY PROUD. BUT NOW LITTLE OWL YOU MUST PREPARE YOURSELF FOR YOUR NEXT ADVENTURE."

Omicron held his head up high. "What must I do?" he asked.

"ALL WILL BECOME CLEAR SOON ENOUGH," Zeus replied. "THE JOURNEY IS VERY TREACHEROUS AND YOU WILL ENCOUNTER MANY DANGERS."

Omicron blinked, "I will do my best Lord Zeus."

"VERY GOOD," Zeus boomed. "NOW SAY GOODBYE TO YOUR FRIENDS."

Omicron turned to Delphina. "Farewell high priestess," he hooted and nuzzled her hand with his metal head.

"I won't forget you Omicron," Delphina

sobbed, stroking the owl's bronze feathers.

Perimos pretended to smile but his twinkling eyes glistened with tears. "Good luck my friend," he patted Omicron. "May the gods be with you."

Omicron whirled his head around in acknowledgment, then fluttered up to the statue of Zeus and perched himself on the god's knee.

"I am ready," he said boldly.

"SO BE IT," Zeus's voice grew faint as Omicron closed his eyes and thought of Athena. In a flash, lighting shot out from the tip of Zeus' spear and the owl disappeared in a clap of thunder.

The last thing that Omicron saw was Delphina waving sadly to him before he was swept up in a ball of light. His quest to prove his worth to the gods and return to Mount Olympus continued…

Look out for Omicron's next mythological

adventure...

COMING SOON!

THE OLYMPIANS

ZEUS: King of the Gods, God of the Sky.

HERA: Queen of the Gods, Goddess of Marriage and Family.

POSEIDON: God of the Seas, Earthquakes and Waves.

ATHENA: Goddess of Wisdom, Crafts and Warfare.

ARES: God of War.

APHRODITE: Goddess of Love and Beauty.

APOLLO: God of Light, Knowledge, Music and Poetry.

ARTEMIS: Goddess of the Hunt.

HERMES: Messenger of the Gods.

DEMETER: Goddess of Fertility, Agriculture and Nature.

HEPHAESTUS: Blacksmith of the Gods, God of Fire.

HESTIA: Goddess of the Hearth and Domesticity.

DIONYSUS: God of Wine.

HADES: Lord of the Underworld.

ACKNOWLEDGEMENTS

Huge thanks to all my family and friends who followed and advised Omicron on his journey from first draft to final cut. Karen, Stefano, Georgina you're amazing! Special thanks also to my fabulous cover designer Fiona and my scrupulous editor A.B.

Most importantly, thank you to my sister Christiana for putting HB, 2B and 3B pencils to paper and helping me to illustrate Omicron's first adventure.

Together we can most certainly climb any mountain. Even Mount Olympus!

Printed in Poland
by Amazon Fulfillment
Poland Sp. z o.o., Wrocław

50783150R00059